The Berenstain Bears
and The
BULLY

If a cub gets beat up,
that's usually when
he/she vows to make sure
it doesn't happen again.

A FIRST TIME BOOK®

The Berenstain Bears
and The
BULLY

Stan & Jan Berenstain

Random House 🏠 New York

Copyright © 1993 by Berenstain Enterprises, Inc. All rights reserved. Published in the United States by Random House Children's Books, a division of Random House, Inc., New York. Random House and the colophon are registered trademarks of Random House, Inc. First Time Books and the colophon are registered trademarks of Berenstain Enterprises, Inc. randomhouse.com/kids   BerenstainBears.com

Library of Congress Cataloging-in-Publication Data
Berenstain, Stan. The Berenstain Bears and the bully / Stan and Jan Berenstain.
p. cm. — (First time books) Summary: When she takes a beating from the class bully,
Sister Bear learns a valuable lesson in self-defense—and forgiveness.
ISBN 978-0-679-84805-9 (pbk.) — ISBN 978-0-307-97889-9 (ebook)
[1. Bears—Fiction. 2. Bullies—Fiction. 3. Assertiveness (Psychology)—Fiction.] I. Berenstain, Jan.
II. Title. III. Series: Berenstain, Stan. First time books. PZ7.B4483Bec 1993 [E]—dc20 92-45875
Printed in the United States of America   45 44 43 42 41 40 39 38 37

One day, Mama, Papa, and Brother Bear were busy in the yard when Sister Bear came home crying. Her face was scratched and dirty, and her clothes were torn. "What happened to you?" asked Mama.

"Please tell us," said Papa.

Brother couldn't believe how beat-up Sister looked. Her jumper and blouse were torn. Her face and fur were a mess. Even her pink bow was drooping.

"Did you fall?" asked Mama. Sister shook her head no.

"Was there an accident?" asked Papa. Once again she shook her head no.

"I think I can tell you what happened,"
said Brother. "It looks to me like somebody
beat her up."

"Beat her up? That's outrageous!" said Papa.

"Who in the world would beat up a sweet
little cub like Sister?" asked Mama.

"A bully might," said Brother.

That's when Sister stopped crying long enough to get some words out. "B-B-Brother's right," she sobbed. "A no-good nasty rotten bully beat me up—*and for no reason!*" Just the thought of it made her so angry that she started to cry all over again.

Mama and Papa helped Sister up the steps and into the house. After a drink of water, she calmed down enough to tell them what had happened.

"Lizzy, Queenie, and I were playing tag at the playground when this new cub—a no-good bully named Tuffy—stuck out a foot and tripped me. So I got up and said, 'Why don't you watch where you put your feet?' Before I knew what was happening, it was POW, BAM, WHAMMO, and I was flat on my back with this Tuffy character sitting on my chest rubbing dirt in my face."

"Outrageous!" roared Papa. "Where's my hat? I'm going over to that playground and—" Mama pulled Papa aside.

"You're going to do no such thing," she said.

"But something has to be done," Papa said.

"Indeed, it does," agreed Mama. "But right now we have to take care of Sister." She turned to call, "Brother! Would you please get me a wet washclo— Where's Brother?"

"Don't know," said Sister. "He was here one minute, and the next minute he was gone."

Lizzy and Queenie were still at the playground when Brother got there. "I've got a knuckle sandwich for some bully named Tuffy," he said. "Where is he?"

"Brother," said Lizzy, "I think there's something you ought to—"

"Never mind the small talk," he growled. "Just point him out and get out of the way!"

Lizzy shrugged and pointed to the small building that housed the Boys' Room and the Girls' Room.

But there was no one there. No one, that is, but a little girl who was coming out of the Girls' Room.

But hold everything! The little girl
was wearing a T-shirt that said *Tuffy!*
"*YOU'RE TUFFY?*" said Brother.
"Yeah," she said. "Wanna make somethin' out of it?"
"But—but you're a *girl!*" said Brother.
"What did you expect me to be—an eggplant?" said Tuffy.
Brother Bear was shocked right down to his very bones.
The big bully he was going to clean up
the playground with was not only a girl,
but a little girl at that. Maybe even a bit
smaller than Sister.

When Lizzy and Queenie came over to watch, Tuffy figured out who Brother was. "Hey!" she said. "You must be the big brother of Little Miss Pink Hairbow! She got fresh, so I cleaned her clock. Wanna make somethin' out of it?"

That was exactly what Brother wanted to do. But there was no way he could hit a girl. If he did, then *he'd* be the bully. It was all he could do to turn away and leave.

"Chicken! Just like your sister!" yelled Tuffy. Brother headed home, hands in pockets, staring at the ground.

Something had to be done! But what? As he passed the school, Brother got an idea. But he would have to hurry. It was Friday afternoon, and the school would be closing for the weekend. He hoped Mr. Grizzmeyer, the gym teacher, hadn't left yet.

When Brother got home, he was carrying something in a big bag.

Instead of going in the front door, he quietly opened the side hatch and dropped the bag into the cellar. Then he closed the hatch and rejoined the family by going in the front door.

"Where have you been?" asked Mama. "We've been having a family meeting."

"Er—I was just checking out the playground," Brother said.

"And no doubt you found out that Tuffy is a girl," said Mama. "We've been discussing the situation and have pretty much decided that the best thing for Sister to do is simply to avoid this awful Tuffy person. Then, too, you'll be at school, and you can keep an eye on Sister. What do you think of the plan?"

"It's okay," said Brother. "But Sister's
the one that got beat up. What does she think?"

"It's okay, I guess," said Sister. "But what
I'd really like to do is punch that Tuffy's
nose right through her face,
then kick her in the shin,
then knock her down and—"

"Now, Sister," said Mama,
"we've been through all that."

Good! thought Brother.
Sister and I are on the
same wavelength.

Before dinner, Brother passed Sister a note. It said, "Important! Meet me in the cellar at seven o'clock."

The first thing Sister saw when she showed up for the secret meeting was one of Mama's big bags of dried beans sitting on a stool. There was a drawing of a face marked *Tuffy* taped to it, and Brother was standing beside it holding the bag he had gotten at school. He also had a book.

"What's this all about?" asked Sister.

"It's about that Tuffy character, and you not getting beat up again," Brother said.

"Sounds good so far," said Sister.

"Mama's bag of beans is a punching bag," Brother said.

"A punching bag named Tuffy," said Sister. "Perfect!" She gave the beans a pretty good punch.

"Not bad," said Brother.

What's in the other bag?" Sister asked.

"Boxing gloves," Brother said. "And this book is called *The Art of Self-Defense*."

"Where did you get all this stuff?" asked Sister.

"From Mr. Grizzmeyer. I told him I had a friend who was having trouble with a bully. We've got it just for the weekend. It goes back Monday morning."

"Then what are we waiting for?" Sister said. "LET'S GET STARTED!"

Sister turned out to be a good
student of the art of self-defense.
With Brother's help, she learned—

the left jab,

the right cross,

the left hook,

and the uppercut.

She also learned to duck.

And she punched Mama's
dried beans silly.

"Well, you learned quite
a lot over the weekend,"
Brother said on Monday morning.
"But there's something very
important for you to remember:
You still have to avoid Tuffy!
She's a mean little thing.
She was even ready to take
me on!"

"Don't worry," said Sister.
"I can still feel where she
socked me on the jaw."

Sister did a good job of avoiding
Tuffy. She avoided her all day
Monday,

and all day Tuesday.

But at recess on Wednesday, Tuffy did something so mean and nasty that Sister just had to do something. *Tuffy was throwing stones at a baby bird that couldn't fly yet!* "Stop that, you bully!" shouted Sister. "You'll hurt that baby bird!"

CHIRP
CHIR

"Well, if it isn't Little Miss Pink Hairbow!" said Tuffy. "You know somethin'? I'd much rather hurt you!"

She rushed at Sister with her hard little fists ready.

But Sister was ready, too. She had her left out and her right up, protecting her jaw. When Tuffy threw a hard right, Sister ducked, then hit her square on the nose with a right cross.

That quickly, Tuffy found herself sitting on the ground with a bloody nose.

And almost that quickly, one of the recess teachers swooped down on Sister and Tuffy, pulled them into school, and sat them on the principal's discipline bench.

Sister's mind was a blurry mix of pride that she had protected the baby bird and shock that she was sitting on the principal's famous discipline bench. But she was even more shocked when she saw that Tuffy was crying. "What are you crying about? I only hit you once," Sister said.

"I'm not crying about that," said Tuffy.

"Then what *are* you crying about?" Sister couldn't help wondering what could make a cub as tough and mean as Tuffy cry.

MR. HONEYCOMB PRINCIPAL

"If the principal tells my mom and dad about this," said Tuffy, "I won't be able to sit down for a—well, a long time."

Hmm, thought Sister. Here's a cub who maybe gets hit a lot at home. Maybe that's why she likes to hit other cubs at school. But Sister didn't think about that for long.

She was too worried
about what was going
to happen to her.
Mr. Honeycomb, the
principal, was very strict
about fighting.

The way it turned out, one of the other recess teachers had seen the whole thing and told Mr. Honeycomb that Sister was just trying to protect a baby bird. So Mr. Honeycomb let Sister off with a warning.

As for Tuffy, the principal didn't call in her parents. But she did lose a week of recess, and she had to visit the school psychologist twice a week for quite a while.